Dear Parent:

Psst . . . you're looking at the Super Secret Weapon of Reading. It's called comics.

STEP INTO READING® COMIC READERS are a perfect step in learning to read. They provide visual cues to the meaning of words and helpfully break out short pieces of dialogue into speech balloons.

Here are some terms commonly associated with comics:
 PANEL: A section of a comic with a box drawn around it.
 CAPTION: Narration that helps set the scene.
 SPEECH BALLOON: A bubble containing dialogue.
 GUTTER: The space between panels.

Tips for reading comics with your child:

• Have your child read the speech balloons while you read the captions.
• Ask your child: What is a character feeling? How can you tell?
• Have your child draw a comic showing what happens after the book is finished.

STEP INTO READING® COMIC READERS are designed to engage and to provide an empowering reading experience. They are also fun. The best-kept secret of comics is that they create lifelong readers. **And that will make you the real hero of the story!**

Jenn — *M. Holm*

Jennifer L. Holm and Matthew Holm
Co-creators of the Babymouse and Squish series

Special thanks to Michelle Cogan, Nicole Corse, Venetia Davie, Ryan Ferguson, Sarah Lazar, Charnita Belcher, Dani Light, Tanya Mann, Gabrielle Miles, Dan Mokriy, Allison Monterosso, Julia Phelps, Andrew Tan, David Wiebe, Sharon Woloszyk, and ARC Productions.

Published in the United States by Random House Children's Books, a division of Random House LLC, 1745 Broadway, New York, NY 10019, and in Canada by Random House of Canada Limited, Toronto, Penguin Random House Companies.

Visit us on the Web!
StepIntoReading.com
randomhousekids.com

Educators and librarians, for a variety of teaching tools, visit us at
RHTeachersLibrarians.com

ISBN 978-0-553-50745-4 (trade) — ISBN 978-0-375-97407-6 (lib. bdg.) — ISBN 978-0-553-50746-1 (ebook)

Printed in the United States of America   10 9 8 7 6

Barbie Life in the Dreamhouse

Cupcake Challenge

A COMIC READER

Adapted by Mary Tillworth

Based on the screenplay by Robin J. Stein

Random House 🏠 New York

The stage is set.
The lights go on.
The show is about to begin!

The podium appears.

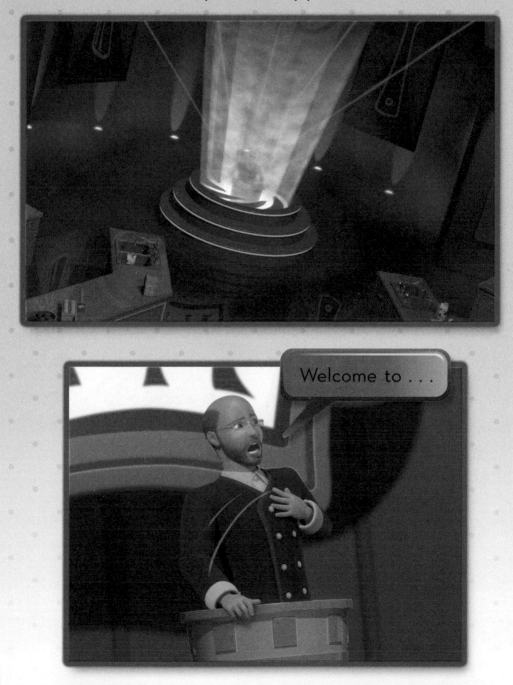

Welcome to . . .

Ryan gets a taste of Raquelle's outrageous personality.

A few minutes later . . .

Teresa's cupcakes are in the oven first!

Barbie wants just a taste. . . .

Barbie just wants one tiny taste.

Awww . . .

Stop thinking about it!

Thwack!

Meanwhile, Raquelle gets a call from her agent.

How could I not get that acting part? I sent in a four-hour audition tape!

Barbie, Teresa, Ryan, Chef Jean, and monkey can't believe it.

Dessert down!

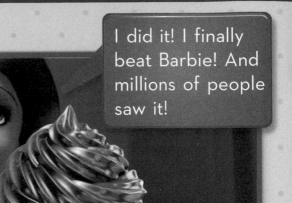

I did it! I finally beat Barbie! And millions of people saw it!

Millions? Ha! I wish! We're on at the same time as *Life in the Dreamhouse.*

Nobody watches *this* show!